Jodorowsky   Gimenez

The Metabarons™

Blood and Steel

Jodorowsky   Gimenez

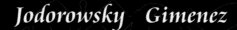

The Metabarons™

Blood and Steel

ORIGINAL METABARON CHARACTER CREATED
BY MŒBIUS AND JODOROWSKY

STORY BY
ALEXANDRO JODOROWSKY

ART, COLOR & COVER BY
JUAN GIMENEZ

ENGLISH TRANSLATION BY
**JULIA SOLIS, KATHLEEN JANICK
& JUSTIN KELLY**

EDITED BY
**PHILIPPE HAURI
& BRUNO LECIGNE**

ADDITIONAL BOOK TEXT
**ADRIAN A. CRUZ
& IAN SATTLER**

LOGOS DESIGNED BY
DIDIER GONORD

COLLECTION DESIGNED BY
THIERRY FRISSEN

Humanoids Publishing ™

Chairman & Publisher
FABRICE GIGER

Literary Director
PHILIPPE HAURI

Director of Publishing U.S.
DAVE OLBRICH

Director of Finance and Administration
PAM SHRIVER

Managing Editor
ADRIAN A. CRUZ

Marketing Manager
IAN SATTLER

Graphic Designer
THIERRY FRISSEN

Circulation
SUE HARTUNG

Licensing & Development
JUSTIN CONNOLLY

PUBLISHED BY
HUMANOIDS PUBLISHING™
(in association with Les Humanoïdes Associés)
PO Box 931658 Hollywood, CA 90093

ISBN 1-930652-24-0
First Printing October 2001

This book collects the stories originally published in English as
The Metabarons #6-10 by Humanoids Publishing.

THE STORY SO FAR

The saga of the Metabarons begins with Baron Othon Van Salza, heir to the Castaka legacy. Through a cruel twist of fate, Othon has become a solitary warrior, unable to father children. He has unlimited wealth but no family to share it with. Dedicating his life to the art of fighting and the study of weapons technology, Othon hones his skills as Supreme Warrior.

When the Imperial embryo is kidnapped, Othon volunteers to save the precious zygote, once again proving himself in battle and earning the title of METABARON. As a reward for his loyal service, the Imperial Family sends him a Shabda-Oud Priestess, Honorata, to take as wife. Through Honorata's magic, Othon is able to impregnate his new wife despite his previous castration. During an assassination attempt on Honorata in her last trimester of pregnancy, the couple's unborn son is injected with a modicum of Epyphite. The Epyphite's gravity-defying properties somehow fuse with the child in utero, making him weightless upon birth.

Mad with grief over his apparently crippled son, Othon wants to kill the infant Aghnar, whom he believes will never be worthy of the Castaka legacy. But Honorata and Othon strike a deal. Honorata will take Aghnar, raise him in the wilderness and train him to be a fierce warrior. On his seventh birthday they will return to Othon's fortress, at which time Othon will test the boy. If Aghnar proves worthy of the Castakas' lineage, Othon will accept him as son despite his disability.

When the time comes, Aghnar proves stronger than either Othon or Honorata could have hoped, even going as far as to sacrifice his own feet to pass the test. Othon welcomes his family back into his house and arms. By fashioning cybernetic feet for his son, Othon establishes the Metabarons' tradition of mutilation and cybernetics.

When Aghnar turns thirteen, Honorata confesses that she had been sent to Othon by her Shabda-Oud superiors with the secret plan of bearing a hermaphrodite child (and therefore a possible heir to the Imperial Throne). Her love for Othon forced the idea from her mind but now, on her son's thirteenth birthday, her superiors expect her to deliver the promised hermaphrodite. Othon fashions a plan, and when the Shabda-Oud Whore-Priestesses arrive to collect the child, they are exterminated and their organic space ship destroyed. The victory is not without its cost however, as Honorata's betrayal has made her family vulnerable to retaliation and they must leave their planet. Honorata delivers her final confession; she cannot go with them. When she was sent to Othon, her cybernetic heart was secretly implanted with a bomb so that she could never leave the planet or abandon her mission. With Shabda-Oud Cetacyborgs already on the way, Othon and Aghnar are forced to leave Honorata to die in the impending explosion of her heart-bomb. As they watch their home disintegrate, and Honorata with it, Othon makes Aghnar vow to take vengeance on the Shabda-Oud for their treachery.

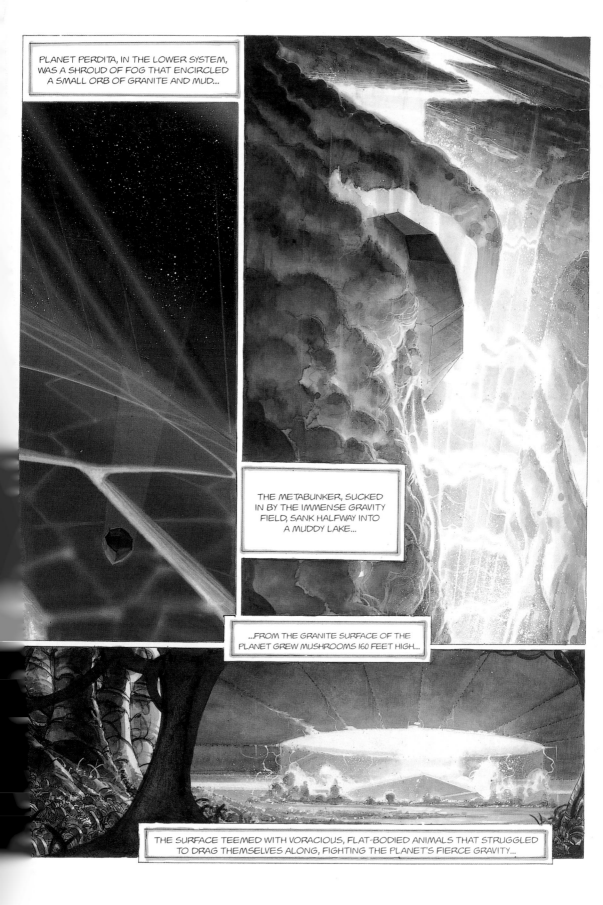

PLANET PERDITA, IN THE LOWER SYSTEM, WAS A SHROUD OF FOG THAT ENCIRCLED A SMALL ORB OF GRANITE AND MUD...

THE METABUNKER, SUCKED IN BY THE IMMENSE GRAVITY FIELD, SANK HALFWAY INTO A MUDDY LAKE...

...FROM THE GRANITE SURFACE OF THE PLANET GREW MUSHROOMS 160 FEET HIGH...

THE SURFACE TEEMED WITH VORACIOUS, FLAT-BODIED ANIMALS THAT STRUGGLED TO DRAG THEMSELVES ALONG, FIGHTING THE PLANET'S FIERCE GRAVITY...

GIGANTIC APES, IMPERVIOUS
TO THE PULL OF GRAVITY,
LIVED IN THE SUMMITS. THEY FLOATED
DOWN ALONG PALE RAYS OF LIGHT
TO DEVOUR PIECES OF BARK
WHICH THEY PULLED OFF
THE MUSHROOM STALKS...

SOMETIMES, A CHORUS OF STRANGE CRIES
COULD BE HEARD COMING FROM OUTSIDE.
THEN, BREAKING THROUGH THE SPONGY
DOMES, THE DYING APES WOULD PLUMMET
DOWN, HAVING SUDDENLY REGAINED
THEIR WEIGHT...

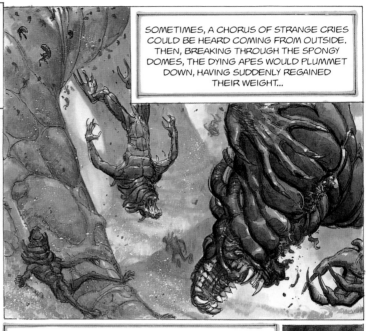

...THEY SMASHED WITHOUT CEREMONY
AGAINST THE GROUND, TO BE IMMEDIATELY
DEVOURED BY THE FLAT CREATURES...

THIS IS PLANET PERDITA, MY SON...
FLAT MONSTERS, FLOATING APES, GIGANTIC
MUSHROOMS, FOG, MUD, GRANITE...
AND NOTHING ELSE... COUGH... COUGH...

YOU COUGH MORE AND MORE
OFTEN, FATHER... I'M VERY WORRIED...

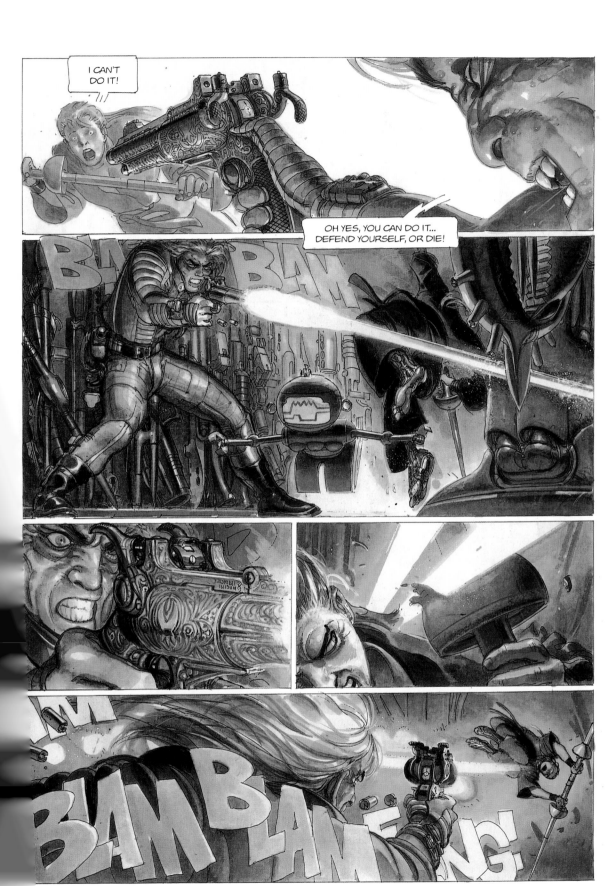

MY ENTIRE BODY IS IMPLANTED WITH OKO MINI-BOMBS... ANYWHERE YOUR WEAPON PIERCES ME, IT WILL SET ONE OFF...
AND YOU WILL BE DISINTEGRATED, ALONG WITH ME AND THE REST OF THE PLANET... SO HOW WILL YOU KILL ME?
THERE MIGHT BE BOOBY TRAPS ALL OVER YOUR BODY... BUT CERTAINLY NOT IN YOUR BRAIN! IF THERE WAS A BOMB IN THERE, YOU WOULDN'T BE ABLE TO SPEAK!
INTELLIGENCE IS THE MOST FORMIDABLE WEAPON! I AM PROUD OF YOUR MENTAL MASTERY! YOU WILL WIPE OUT THE SHABDA-OUD!
AND NOW, FREE ME! SEND ME THROUGH THE DOORS OF DEATH, SO THAT I MAY ATTAIN...
...THE TRUE LIFE!

IF I WERE A DROP OF DEW, I COULD TAKE REFUGE ON A BLADE OF GRASS...

...BUT I AM ONLY A MAN, WITH NO HOME ON ANY PLANET...

THUS BEGAN THE MOST IMPORTANT CASTAKA TRADITION: A METABARON CAN BE CONSIDERED INITIATED ONLY AFTER HE HAS SUCCEEDED IN KILLING HIS OWN FATHER.

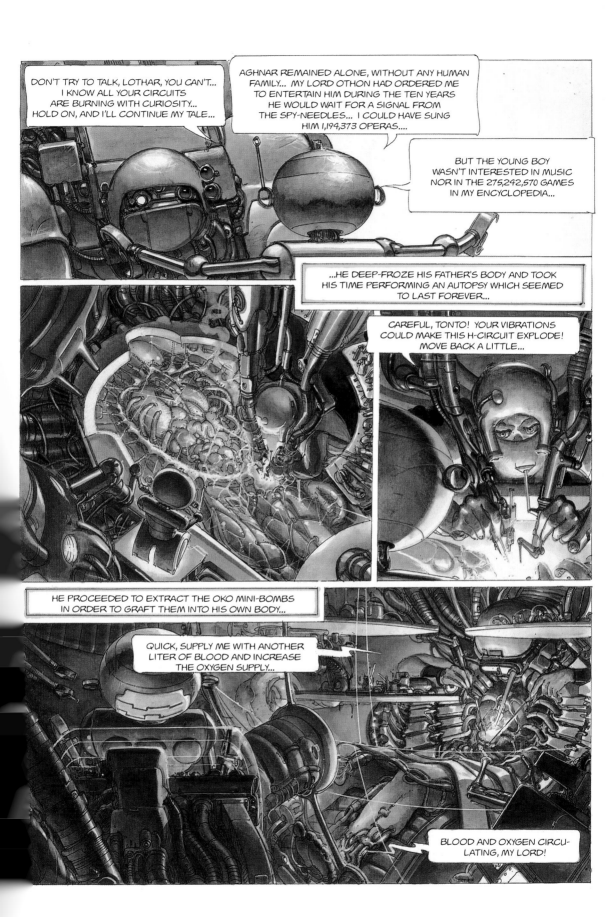

IN HIS RARE MOMENTS
OF RECREATION, HE WOULD
GO FOR WALKS OUTSIDE.
THE FLAT MONSTERS COULD
NOT DEVOUR HIS METAL FEET...

ONE DAY, WHEN HE SAW THE DYING APES FALLING,
HE SHOT ONE WITH AN EPYPHITE-SOAKED DART...

...AND BROUGHT THE WOUNDED CREA-
TURE HOME. I CAN'T SAY I WAS PLEASED
TO SEE HIM RETURN IN SUCH COMPANY.
CLEANING UP THE BIO-SHIT AND PISS
THAT IRRATIONAL ORGANISMS ARE IN
THE HABIT OF DROPPING EVERYWHERE
REPULSES ME...

16

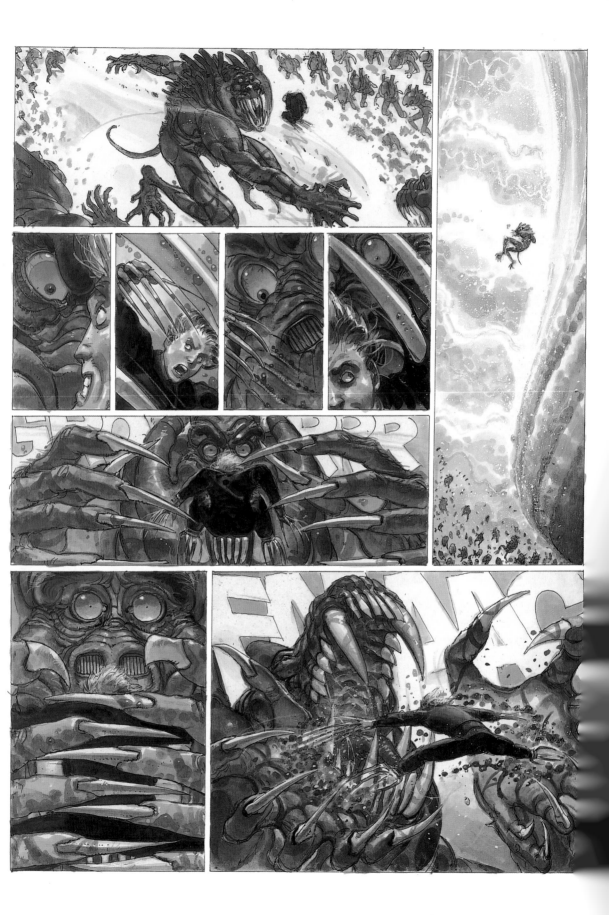

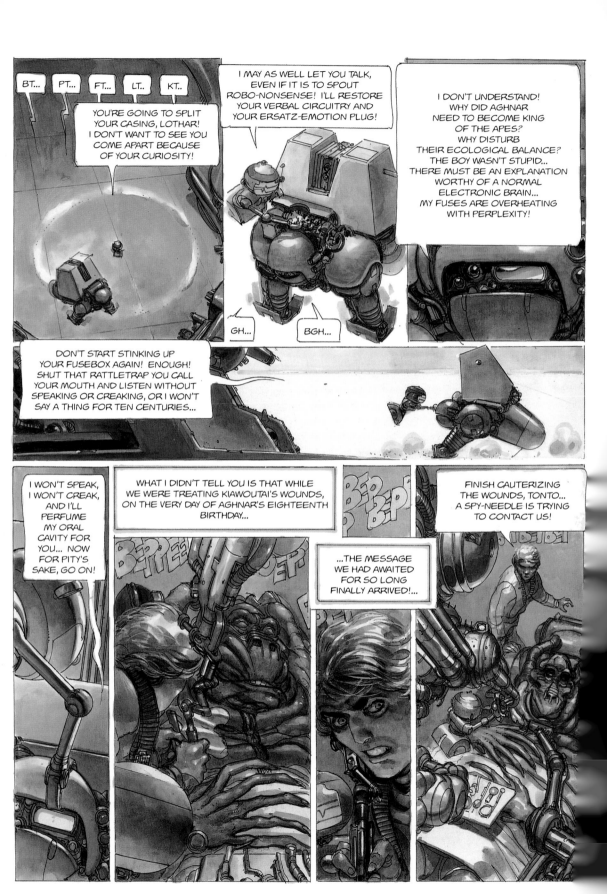

BT... PT... FT... LT... KT..

YOU'RE GOING TO SPLIT YOUR CASING, LOTHAR! I DON'T WANT TO SEE YOU COME APART BECAUSE OF YOUR CURIOSITY!

I MAY AS WELL LET YOU TALK, EVEN IF IT IS TO SPOUT ROBO-NONSENSE! I'LL RESTORE YOUR VERBAL CIRCUITRY AND YOUR ERSATZ-EMOTION PLUG!

I DON'T UNDERSTAND! WHY DID AGHNAR NEED TO BECOME KING OF THE APES? WHY DISTURB THEIR ECOLOGICAL BALANCE? THE BOY WASN'T STUPID... THERE MUST BE AN EXPLANATION WORTHY OF A NORMAL ELECTRONIC BRAIN... MY FUSES ARE OVERHEATING WITH PERPLEXITY!

GH... BGH...

DON'T START STINKING UP YOUR FUSEBOX AGAIN! ENOUGH! SHUT THAT RATTLETRAP YOU CALL YOUR MOUTH AND LISTEN WITHOUT SPEAKING OR CREAKING, OR I WON'T SAY A THING FOR TEN CENTURIES...

I WON'T SPEAK, I WON'T CREAK, AND I'LL PERFUME MY ORAL CAVITY FOR YOU... NOW FOR PITY'S SAKE, GO ON!

WHAT I DIDN'T TELL YOU IS THAT WHILE WE WERE TREATING KIAWOUTAÏ'S WOUNDS, ON THE VERY DAY OF AGHNAR'S EIGHTEENTH BIRTHDAY...

...THE MESSAGE WE HAD AWAITED FOR SO LONG FINALLY ARRIVED!...

FINISH CAUTERIZING THE WOUNDS, TONTO... A SPY-NEEDLE IS TRYING TO CONTACT US!

24

THE SHABDA-OUD WERE LIVING ON AN ICE ASTEROID TRANSFORMED INTO A COMET, GUARDED BY THEIR CETACYBORGS...

DAMNED WHORES! PROTECTED BY THOSE SIX MONSTERS, THEY ARE INVINCIBLE!

I CAN NEVER DESTROY THEM ALL BY MYSELF... VENGEANCE IS BUT A DREAM...

BUT MASTER, WE KNOW FOR A FACT THAT THE WITCHES HAVE SEVEN CETACYBORGS...

A SPY-NEEDLE HAD PICKED IT UP HEADING FOR THE BLUE SOLAR SYSTEM OF BETA-KUNTRI, PILOTED BY THREE ASSASSINS...

THAT'S RIGHT... SO WHERE IS THE SEVENTH?

THEY'RE ON A SECRET MISSION... THAT'S OUR ONLY CHANCE... I HAVE TO FIND A WAY TO GET MY HANDS ON THAT BEAST WITHOUT ALERTING THE ICE ASTEROID!

A LOST CAUSE, MASTER... THERE IS NO WAY TO BEAT A CETACYBORG WITHOUT UNLEASHING AS MUCH FORCE AS AN EXPLODING SUN!

AGHNAR DESPAIRED... UNTIL HE DISCOVERED THE MAGON PROTO-CIVILIZATION... IT WAS NOW ESSENTIAL THAT HE BECOME THEIR PATRIARCH...

THE LEGEND OF THE APES FITS IN PERFECTLY WITH MY PLAN! I HAVE A WAY TO TAKE OVER THE CETACYBORG! I WILL BE ABLE TO AVENGE YOU, MOTHER!

MY MASTER LOADED ALL HIS SUBJECTS INTO THE METABUNKER AND PROMISED TO TAKE THEM TO THE DIAMOND PLANET.

THE APES, WHICH WE HAD INJECTED WITH A HEAT-IMMUNIZING AGENT, WERE IN A TEMPORARY STATE OF COMA. WE CAST THEM INTO SPACE LIKE A TIDE OF DELICIOUS ORGANIC MATTER... I WAS PILOTING THE METABUNKER...

IMPOSSIBLE... OUR CRAFT IS NO LONGER RESPONDING...

BETTER NOT TO FORCE IT... AS SOON AS IT HAS FINISHED SWALLOWING ALL THIS ORGANIC WASTE, WE WILL REGAIN CONTROL...

WHAT AN ABSURD DELAY!

DESPITE THE NEUROLOGICAL COMMANDS, THE BEAST FOLLOWED ITS PRIMEVAL NATURE...

...AND BEGAN SWALLOW-ING THE APES.

AH, LOVE! HOW I WOULD LIKE TO HAVE BETWEEN MY THIGHS A TENDER SHAFT THAT GROWS, HARDENS, STANDS ERECT, THEN ERUPTS!

OR A SMOOTH CANAL, BORDERED WITH HAIR, WHICH BECOMES MOIST! WHAT SUBLIME FOLLY IS THE HUMAN ORGANISM! I DROOL AT THE THOUGHT OF IT! OUR MATHEMATICAL PERFECTION IS SO TEDIOUS!

I'M ONLY ALLOWING THIS INTERRUPTION BECAUSE YOU ARE COMPLETELY RIGHT, LOTHAR. I FIND IT TEDIOUS TOO!

BUT NEVER MIND... I WILL GO ON... TO MAKE A LONG STORY SHORT, IN ORDER TO PREVENT HIS DAUGHTER'S SUICIDE, THE KING HAD TO LET HER DEPART ON A MOTO-CRAFT PILOTED BY AN UNKNOWN HOTHEAD, TAKING ONLY THE CLOTHES ON HER BACK...

ON THE WAY TO THE CETACYBORG, AGHNAR TOLD ODA OF HIS TRAGIC LIFE...

YOU WILL HELP ME CARRY OUT MY REVENGE, ODA!

I WILL DELIVER YOU, BOUND HAND AND FOOT, AS IF I HAD CAPTURED YOU!

YES, AGHNAR...

AFTER I HAVE ANNIHILATED THOSE WITCHES, WE WILL GO AND LIVE ON A DISTANT PLANET, WHERE NO ONE KNOWS WHO WE ARE. WE WILL RAISE A NORMAL FAMILY, FAR AWAY FROM THIS AWFUL EMPIRE...

YES, AGHNAR...

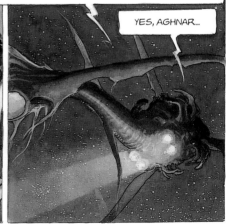

...ANY MOMENT. WHAT? ...LOTHAR! ...MASTER? ...OH, NO

WHEW, HE DISAPPEARED JUST IN TIME! FORTUNATELY BIO-ELECTROGRAMS ONLY SPEND 3:05.07 IN A SOLID STATE BEFORE DISSOLVING!

...AND ALSO BECAUSE YOU CAN BE REBUILT QUICKLYBY THE ANT-ROBOTS, YOU MORONIC HUNK OF JUNK!

TO THINK THAT I ALMOST HAD TO SPEND THE NEXT 35,000 YEARS, 6 MONTHS, 2 WEEKS, 4 DAYS, 5 HOURS, AND 20:12.03 OF MY REMAINING LIFE WITHOUT YOU... WHAT DID YOU DO TO THE METABARON!?

I JUST ASKED HIM: "HOW COULD YOU, MASTER, THE INVINCIBLE WARRIOR, HAVE BEEN WOUNDED AT THE AGE OF 30 YEARS, 2 MONTHS, 3 HOURS, AND 20:04.00, AS INDICATED BY THE SCAR ACROSS YOUR RIGHT EYEBROW?"

MECHANICAL MORON! YOU JUST HAD TO POKE YOUR RUSTY METAL NOSE INTO HIS ONLY SORE SPOT! YOU DESERVE TO HAVE A PALEO-DOG COME AND CHEW UP ALL OF YOUR CIRCUITS!

BUT HOW COULD I KNOW, TONTO? YESTERDAY I ASKED YOU THE SAME QUESTION, AND YOU DIDN'T ANSWER ME!

LOTHAR, YOU CHEATER! I LET YOU CHOOSE BETWEEN FINDING OUT THE REASON BEHIND THAT SCAR, OR HEARING THE REST OF THE METABARONS' HISTORY. AND YOU KNOW WHICH ONE YOU CHOSE...

OHMY-OHMY-OHMY! TONTO, HOW CAN HE POSSIBLY DEFEAT ALL THOSE WITCHES SINGLE-HANDED? YIPES! I WISH I HAD ONE OF THOSE RUBBERY ORGANS THAT HUMANS CALL A BLADDER SO I COULD PISS MYSELF IN FEAR! KEEP GOING, KEEP GOING!

LISTEN, LOTHAR, I'LL CONTINUE THE STORY, BUT IF YOU INTERRUPT ME ONE MORE TIME, I'LL ACTIVATE THE CURRENT METABARON'S BIO-ELECTROGRAM! THIS TIME HE'LL DISINTEGRATE YOU COMPLETELY, YOU HYSTERICAL SCRAP-HEAP!

GULP!

THANKS TO THE PSYCHO-MIMETICS YOU TAUGHT ME, MOTHER, I CAN GET PAST THEIR MENTAL PROBES! YET THANKS TO YOUR TEACHINGS, FATHER, I KNOW THAT NO ILLUSION LASTS FOREVER.

HAIL JEJOH, FULL OF GRACE... BLESSED IS THE SEED YOU CARRY IN YOUR TESTICLES!

AMEN!

SUBDUE YOUR PANIC, MY LOVE, HOLD ON FOR A FEW MORE SECONDS!

NOOOOO! DIRTY MONSTER! AAAAHHH!

MAY SAMA-WAJD BE CONCEIVED! O JEJOH, BRING US THE CHOSEN ONE!

YOU FILTHY OLD HAGS! IF YOU DON'T TAKE THIS HORROR AWAY FROM ME AT ONCE, I'LL HOLD. MY BREATH UNTIL I DIE!...

HEE, HEE, HEEHEEHEE!

TOO LATE NOW, MY PRETTY!

I CAN'T BEAR THIS ANYMORE! SAVE ME, AGHNAR!...

CONFOUND IT! ODA REVEALED MY PRESENCE TOO SOON! NOW EVERYTHING MUST BE RUSHED!

RISE UP, MY DAUGHTERS! A SPY HIDES AMONG US!

QUICKLY! SEND THE ORDERS TO THE CETACYBORG!

AS YOU COMMAND, MASTER!

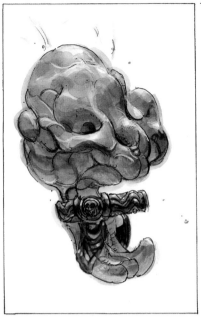

IMPOSSIBLE!!

YOU ARE IMMORTAL...

JEJOH!

TAKE YOUR IMMORTAL!

DON'T BE AFRAID, ODA. IT'S OVER NOW...

THE WITCHES' PSYCHIC POWERS WERE FED BY JEJOH'S BRAINWAVES. WITHOUT HIS ENERGY, THEY BECAME LIKE HEADLESS PALEO-CHICKENS. "TO DEFEAT THE DRAGON WITH A THOUSAND HEADS, PIERCE ITS HEART WITH A SINGLE BLOW!"

YOUR ARM, AGHNAR! YOU'RE LOSING ALL YOUR BLOOD!

ONLY THE STUMP HURTS, ODA.

THE REST OF MY BODY FEELS FINE...

NO INJURY CAN DARKEN MY SPIRIT. IT WILL ALWAYS BE WHOLE. THAT PART OF ME CANNOT BE WOUNDED.

WE, THE ELDERS, ARE NOT ENTIRELY DEPENDENT ON JEJOH. WE ALSO POSSESS OUR OWN POWERS!

WE WILL BURN OUR LAST OUNCE OF ENERGY TO EXTERMINATE YOU, EVIL TRAITOR!

ATTACK ALL... MEAN OLD LADIES!

AGHNAR!

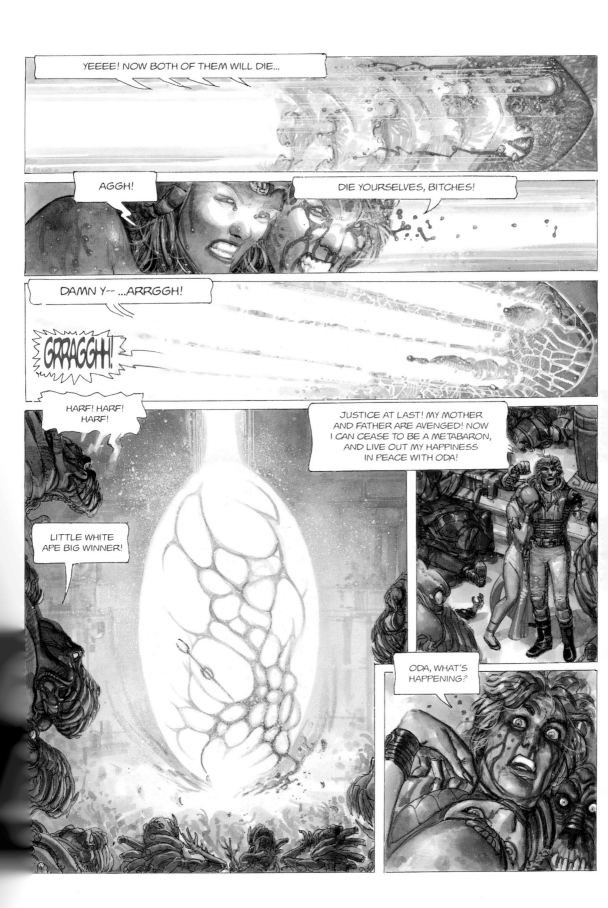

TELL ME TONTO, HOW IS IT THAT YOU, A MACHINE WITH NO KNOWLEDGE OF CEREBRAL BIO-MASS, MANAGED TO PERFORM BRAIN SURGERY ON ODA?

I NEVER OPERATED ON HER! ODA HAD NO NEED FOR BRAIN SURGERY, AS HER SOUL WAS ALREADY EXTINGUISHED. SHE WAS A DEAD SPIRIT, INSIDE A LIVING BODY.

AUUUGGGGHH! THE STRESS IS GOING TO RUIN ALL MY CIRCUITS! SO WHAT HAP-PENED NEXT, TONTO?

IF YOU WANT TO HEAR THE FACTS OF THE MATTER, SHUT THAT GREASY HOLE YOU CALL YOUR FACE AND LISTEN!

FROM SPORES THAT HAD TRAVELED IN THE GOITRES OF THE FEMALE APES, GIGANTIC MUSHROOMS QUICKLY SPRANG UP ACROSS THE SURFACE OF THE ICE ASTEROID. STANDING BESIDE HIS TEN WIVES, KIAWOUTAI WAS OVERCOME WITH BOTH JOY AND SADNESS AS HE BID FAREWELL, PERHAPS FOREVER, TO HIS MESSIAH.

FAREWELL, KIAWOUTAI!

GOOD-BYE, LITTLE WHITE APE. YOU FULFILL PROPHECY: TAKE US FAR FROM FOG WORLD TO HERE, DIAMOND PLANET. THANK YOU, ALWAYS! ALWAYS!

I WON'T LIE TO YOU, ODA. WITHOUT KNOWING THEIR WEAK SPOT, NO ONE CAN DEFEAT SEVEN CETACYBORGS. THEY WILL DEVOUR US!

YOUR BODY STILL BREATHES, BUT YOUR SPIRIT HAS ALREADY DEPARTED FOR THE OTHER WORLD. I WILL FOLLOW YOU GLADLY: IN DEATH WE WILL BE REUNITED.

THE TIME HAS COME! THE END OF THE CLAN OF THE METABARONS! AND I REJOICE IN IT!

HANG ON,
ODA! UGGH!...

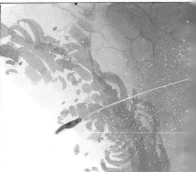

JODOROWSKY
JIMENEZ ©

BUT WHO COULD HAVE DISCOVERED THE SHABDA-OUD SECRET? AND WHY HAS HE COME TO SAVE US? WHAT POWER IS THIS, THAT CAN WIPE OUT SEVEN CETACYBORGS ONE BY ONE?

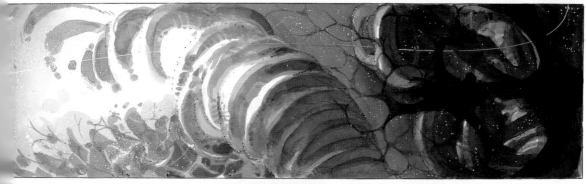

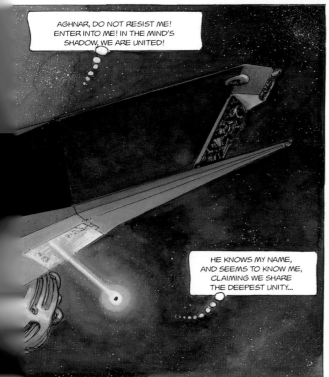

AGHNAR, DO NOT RESIST ME! ENTER INTO ME! IN THE MIND'S SHADOW, WE ARE UNITED!

HE KNOWS MY NAME, AND SEEMS TO KNOW ME, CLAIMING WE SHARE THE DEEPEST UNITY...

HE SAVED MY LIFE... THE LIFE THAT I NO LONGER DESIRE... WHO CAN IT BE?!

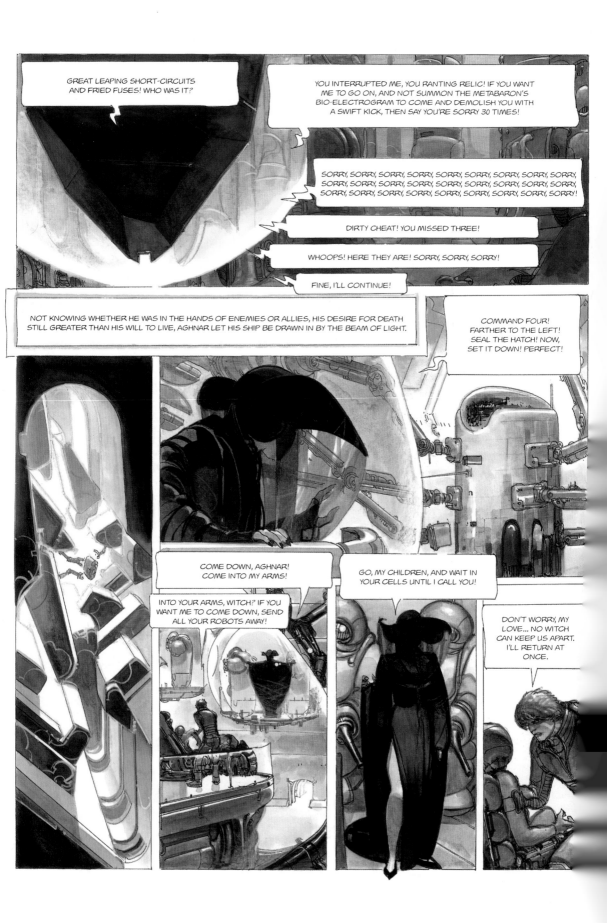

SMELL MY PERFUME, AGHNAR. DO YOU RECOGNIZE IT?

SNIFF...

OH, THAT SCENT!...

OTHON, AGHNAR, PROMISE ME THAT YOU WILL NEVER FORGET THE HYPNOTIC SCENT OF OKHAR'S CARNIVOROUS FLOWERS!

REMEMBER ME...

...AS YOU REMEMBER THOSE FLOWERS!

IT ISN'T POSSIBLE! THOSE ARE THE WORDS MY MOTHER SPOKE BEFORE SHE WENT TO HER DEATH!

I AM NOT DEAD, MY SON! IT'S ME, HONORATA!

STOP, WITCH! I DO NOT BELIEVE YOU! I WITNESSED THE EXPLOSION OF THE BOMB IMPLANTED IN MY MOTHER'S HEART BY YOU DAMNED SHABDA-OUD WHORES!

DARE TO LOOK AT ME, AND LISTEN TO WHAT YOUR BLOOD TELLS YOU!

IMPOSSIBLE! IMPOSSIBLE! IT CAN ONLY BE A HOLO-MASK, A TRUMPED-UP SURFACE HALLUCINATION... WHAT A DASTARDLY TRICK!

8.01 SECONDS LATER, SHE HAD REACHED CHRONO-G, THE PUNCTUAL PRADEX POINT, FOLLOWED BY ALL THE MECA-ROBOTS THAT ACCOMPANIED HER TO THE LABORATORY.

INSIDE THE TEMPORAL FISSURE, HER NEW TIME BEGAN ACCELERATING AT A PHENOMENAL RATE...

...OF WHICH HONORATA AND HER ASSISTANTS WERE ENTIRELY UNAWARE, WRAPPED UP AS THEY WERE IN THEIR PREPARATIONS FOR THE COMPLEX SURGERY.

FOR THEM, TIME SEEMED TO PASS AT NORMAL SPEED. FOR 15 YEARS THEY STUDIED THE HEART-BOMB, UNTIL THEY FINALLY DISCOVERED A WAY TO REMOVE IT WITHOUT TRIGGERING THE EXPLOSION.

MY BRAIN IS ENTERING ALPHA... MY DESIRE IS FADING... IN DELTA, EMOTIONS DISSOLVE... EVEN DEEPER, WORDS DISAPPEAR... NOTHINGNESS.

...WHEN HONORATA HAD ATTAINED A STATE OF PSYCHO-CELLULAR CATALEPSY...

...THEY RISKED THE PERILOUS OPERATION. PERILOUS NOT ONLY BECAUSE OF THE BOMB, BUT ALSO BECAUSE FOR 13 HOURS AND 15:26.12, HONORATA LAY WITH HER CHEST CAVITY OPEN AND HER BLOOD-FLOW INTERRUPTED...

THE OPERATION WAS A COMPLETE SUCCESS. HER NEW HEART, A MAGNIFICENT ORGAN OF ARCTUREAN KATRIANE, BEGAN TO BEAT.

THE NEXT FIVE YEARS WERE SPENT BUILDING A VESSEL CAPABLE OF WITHSTANDING THE VENGEANCE OF THE SHABDA-OUD: NUCLEAR DETONATION OF THE OFFENDING HEART, AND ANNIHILATION OF THE ENTIRE PLANET!

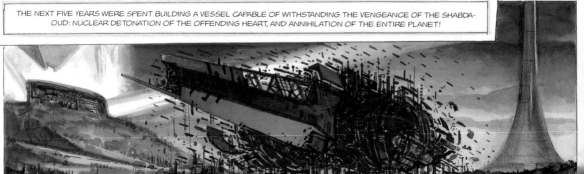

WE WILL AVENGE YOUR MOTHER!

YES, FATHER! WE WILL AVENGE HER!

REMORSE FILLS ME TO THE DEPTHS OF MY SOUL, MY LOVES. YOU MUST BEAR THE PAIN OF MY PRESUMED DEATH UNTIL YOU EXTINGUISH THE SHABDA-OUD FORCES. WHAT IMMENSE SAC-RIFICE IS NECESSARY FOR THE GLORY OF OUR CLAN!

BUT WHY HAVEN'T YOU SHOWN ANY SIGN OF LIFE THESE PAST TEN YEARS? DO YOU HAVE ANY IDEA OF HOW MUCH SUFFERING YOU CAUSED?...

TRY TO UNDERSTAND. I KNEW THAT YOUR FATHER WAS GOING TO DIE. WITHOUT HIM REALIZING IT, MY PSYCHIC SONAR HAD PROBED HIS INJURED LUNGS. BUT AS FOR YOU, YOU HAD TO LIVE!

AT THAT AGE, BELIEVING MY MOTHER DEAD WAS NO LIFE AT ALL! IT WAS PERPETUAL AGONY!

THE ONE WHO IS CRYING IS THE CHILD WHO STILL LIVES WITHIN YOU. OVERCOME HIM! IT IS THE ADULT WHO MUST HEAR MY WORDS: I COULD CONCEAL MY EXISTENCE, WHILE YOU COULD NOT.

YOUR EMOTIONS WOULD HAVE BETRAYED YOU! THE ELDERS WOULD HAVE QUICKLY DETECTED IT, AND IMMEDIATELY WIPED US OUT...

FOR THAT SAME REASON, IT WAS NECESSARY THAT YOU BE HARDENED BY YOUR HATE AND DESIRE FOR REVENGE, SO THAT YOU WOULD PRE-PARE TO EXTERMI-NATE ALL THE SHABDA-OUD ON YOUR OWN.

NOW I'M CERTAIN YOU HAVE A MECHANICAL HEART! YOU DON'T KNOW WHAT IT IS TO SUFFER! COME WITH ME TO MY SHIP...

68

ENOUGH ARGUING, YOU WILL DO AS YOU DESIRE. NOW GO! I MUST GATHER MY STRENGTH IN ORDER TO RETURN CONSCIOUSNESS TO THE ONE WHO WILL BE MOTHER OF YOUR SON!

OF MY SON, YOU SAY? NO! OF MY CHILDREN – BOTH SONS AND DAUGHTERS!

FOOLISH MAN! THE OPERATION WILL BE A LONG ONE: YOU'LL HAVE TIME TO INSTALL YOUR NEW PROTONIC ARM!

WOO-HOO! YEE-HA! WHAT BIO-DELIGHT! A HAPPY ENDING! STOP THERE, TONTO, I'LL GUESS THE REST: HONORATA WILL AWAKEN ODA FROM HER COMA. THEN, ODA WILL LUBRICATE HER LOWER CYLINDER TO RECEIVE AGHNAR'S REPRODUCTIVE PISTON, AND LATER PRODUCE THE GRANDFATHER OF OUR CURRENT METABARON. HALLELUJAH!

CAN IT, ROBO-CLOD! IT WAS MORE LIKE A BIO-TRAGEDY THAN A 'HAPPY ENDING'! SOMETHING AWFUL HAPPENED AND, WHAT'S EVEN WORSE, I WAS AN ACCOMPLICE TO THE CATASTROPHE.

FINISHED? YOU'VE TAKEN AN ETERNITY GRAFTING THIS PROTONIC ARM! HURRY, I WANT TO SEE IF MY MOTHER HAS MANAGED TO AWAKEN MY ODA!

HONORATA? STOP, STAY WHERE YOU ARE! DON'T SAY A WORD! DON'T TELL ME THAT THE OPERATION WAS A FAILURE! I REFUSE TO HEAR THOSE FATAL WORDS!

THE SUTURE IS COMPLETE. THE 'ETERNITY' ONLY LASTED 32:16.0 – A RECORD TIME, MASTER.

TUMP

AGHNAR!

ODA!...

THEIR NAMES WERE THE ONLY WORDS THEY MANAGED TO SPEAK...

SO NOW YOU KNOW?

YES! YOU ARE NOT ODA! ODA IS DEAD! YOU ARE HONORATA! THE SORCERESS WHO STOLE THE BODY OF MY WIFE!

AND ALSO YOUR MOTHER, AGHNAR!

LYING WITCH! WHY DID YOU TELL ME THAT YOU WERE GOING TO OPERATE ON ODA IF YOU HAD DECIDED TO CLONE YOURSELF WITHIN HER?

I DID IT FOR YOU! TELLING YOU THAT ODA'S BRAIN WAS DEAD WOULD HAVE KILLED YOU. YOU WANTED A SON...

ABOMINATION! THE SON YOU BORE ME IS THE PRODUCT OF INCEST!

ONLY IN YOUR MIND! THIS BODY'S FLESH IS NOT MY OWN!

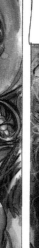

YES IT IS, YOU WICKED VAM- PIRE! NOTHING IS LEFT OF ODA! YOUR SPIRIT INHABITS EVERY ONE OF HER CELLS! WITH YOUR FALSE WORDS OF LOVE, YOU TRICKED ME INTO FATHERING A MONSTER! NOW IT MUST BE ELIMINATED!

NEVER! OUR SON IS THE FULFILL- MENT OF YOUR FATHER OTHON'S GLORIOUS DREAM! THE CLAN OF THE METABARONS MUST LIVE ON, NO MATTER WHAT!

GIVE HIM TO ME!

BACK, TRAITOR, OR I WON'T BE RESPONSI- BLE FOR WHAT HAPPENS TO YOU!

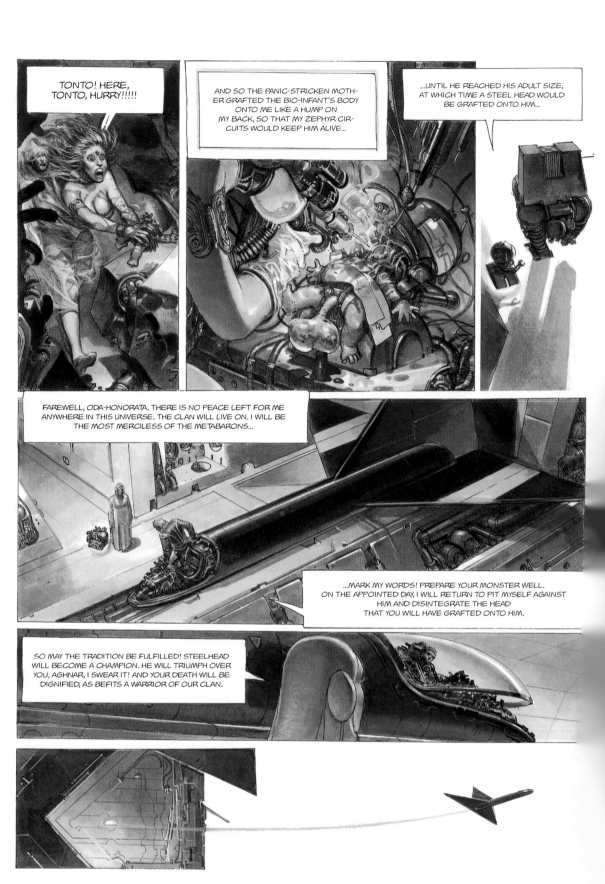

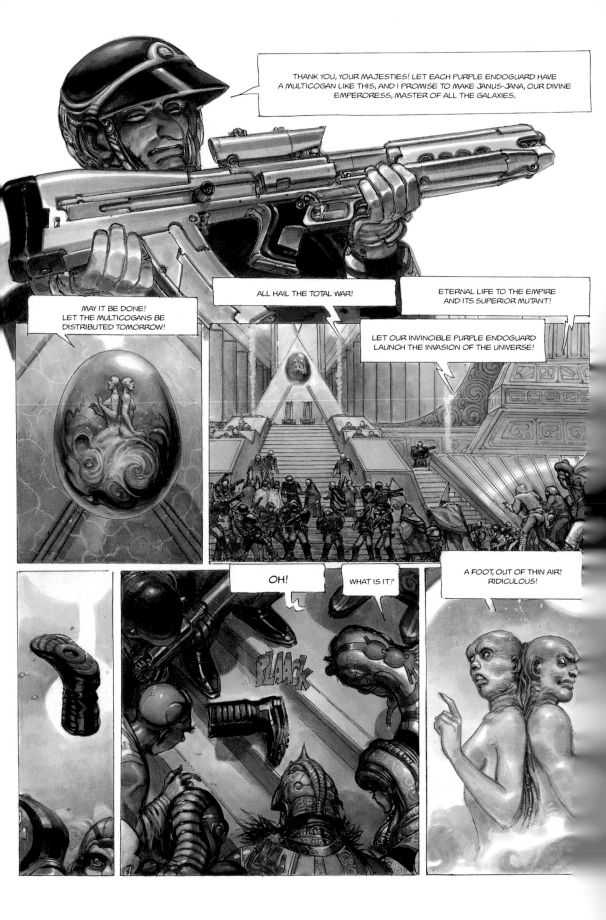

STOP RUNNING LIKE A PAIR OF PALEO-RABBITS ON TERRA PRIMA!

I WIPED OUT THE PURPLE ENDOGUARD TO DEMONSTRATE THE EXTENT OF MY POWERS, BUT I HAVE NOT COME TO MAKE WAR... I HAVE COME TO OFFER MY SERVICES!

I AM THE NEW METABARON!

OH!...

HE'S EVEN MORE POWERFUL THAN HIS PREDECESSOR!

BUT WHAT A SHAMELESS BUNCH OF HYPOCRITICAL CYNICS! HUMANS DON'T EVEN HAVE A MINIMUM OF ROBOT DECENCY!

TOO TRUE! THE AUCTION WENT ON FOR HOURS, EACH GROUP RELENTLESSLY OFFERING FABULOUS SUMS FOR THE PRIVILEGE OF EMPLOYING THE NEW METABARON. OVER THE YEARS, AGHNAR SOLD HIS SERVICES TO THE HIGHEST BIDDER, CHALKING UP VICTORIES FOR CAUSES HE CARED NOTHING ABOUT... HIS BITTERNESS AND CRUELTY BECAME LEGENDARY...

ON PLANET SEC-HUM, HE ASSISTED THE GORDS, DESERT PEOPLE COVERED WITH STINKING SCALES, IN ELIMINATING THE HIREAS, FRAGRANT AQUATIC BEINGS...

IN NIBAL, THE PLANETARY MEGA-CITY, HE LEASED HIMSELF TO THE ZERKOTS, TELEPATHIC SAURIANS, IN ORDER TO CONTAIN THE REVOLUTION OF THE GIANT MACHINES...

HE LED THE PATHETIC TROGLOSOCIALIK ARMADA TO VICTORY OVER THE TRADE SPACE THAT HAD BEEN ENCROACHED UPON BY THE ARROGANT, ARISTOCRATIC CYBERGS...

HE JOINED FORCES WITH ULRITCH THE RED'S PIRATE GANG, HIJACKING A CARGO OF EPIPHYTE
THAT WAS BEING TRANSPORTED BY THREE "MOTHER-COACH" SHIPS...

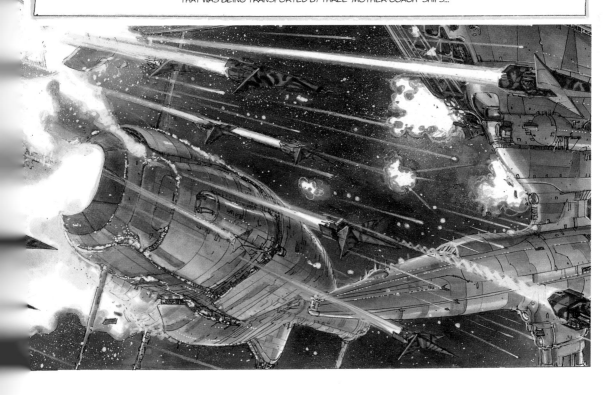

ON JUPITER NOVA, UNDER CONTRACT TO THE EMPERORESS, HE SINGLE-HANDEDLY ELIMINATED, IN THE RECORD TIME OF 8 MINUTES, AN INFANTRY BATTALION OF THREE HUNDRED THOUSAND SCHIZOPHRENICS SUFFERING FROM A CANNIBALISTIC FIT, AS THEY PREPARED TO INVADE THE GOLDEN PLANET AND CONSUME THE FLESH OF JANUS-JANA...

AFTER THE INHABITANTS OF MORGA-THE-BEAUTIFUL HAD DRIED UP THEIR PLANET WITH EXCESSIVE DESIRE TO EXTRACT THE RICHES OF THE GOLDEN EARTH, AGHNAR DIRECTED A CONVOY OF THEIR FLOATING CITIES TOWARDS THE TEFLON SATELLITE, WHERE THEY STAYED TO SETTLE ON THE STERILE LAND. NO VORACIOUS CLAN WOULD EVER DARE ATTACK THEM...

ONE DAY, IN THE REMAINS OF HIS HIDDEN LAIR ON ANASIRMA, THE SACRED MOUNTAIN...

AGHNAR GAZED AT HIMSELF IN A MIRROR...

...AND SAW HIS FATHER'S IMAGE IN THE DARKENED GLASS.

OH, I'VE TRANSFORMED INTO OTHON!

TWENTY YEARS HAD FLOWED BY, TAKING HIS YOUTH WITH THEM.

HE SUDDENLY REALIZED THAT HE WAS AN OLD MAN, CONSUMED BY EMPTINESS.

A GLASS OF GREEN GUANODONT MILK, MASTER?

A WHISKY AND SPV, MASTER?

THIS IS WHAT I'VE COME TO: BETWEEN MASSACRES I GET DRUNK AND LISTEN TO OCTOEL, THE SUPER-MORONIC ROMANTIC OCTOPUS OF THE HYPTERTUBE! ENOUGH!

MY EIGHT TENTACLES, MY HEART... MY THOUSAND SUCKERS FOR YOUUUU...

YOU HEAL MY EVERY PAIN... YOUR QUIVER FULL OF KISSES...

THEN, HE TOOK HIS FAVORITE WEAPON, AND WITHOUT THE SLIGHTEST EMOTION, PRESSED IT AGAINST HIS TEMPLE, PREPARING TO DRAW THE TRIGGER.

NO SUICIDE, METABARON! IMPORTANT OFFER FOR YOU!

WHAT THE...?

IMPOSSIBLE! PTHAGUREANS! HOW IN PALEO-HELL DID YOU FIND ME?

FORGIVE HYPERTUBE INTERRUPTION! WE BE PEACE AMBASSADORS! OFFER ONE MILLION BILLION KUBLARS! YOU DEIGN WELCOME US?

ONE MILLION BILLION KUBLARS?!... IS THERE EVEN THAT MUCH MONEY IN ALL THE GALAXY? COME ON IN!

AND SO A BOUNDING PTHAGUREAN VESSEL CROSSED THE INHOSPITABLE, SNOWY EXPANSE, HEADING TOWARDS THE METABARON'S LAIR.

THE PROBLEM IS INSOLUBLE, YOUR MAJESTIES!

FIRE!

AAARRGHKK!

HOW AWFUL!

THAT'S HOW YOU'LL END UP IF YOU DON'T GIVE US A SOLUTION THIS INSTANT! PUT THOSE STINKING CIRCUITS THAT YOU CALL YOUR BRAINS TO WORK!

OUR GALAXY AND THE PTHAGUREAN GALAXY ARE OF EQUAL STRENGTH: IT IS THE METABARON ALONE WHO TIPS THE SCALES IN FAVOR OF THE INVADER. WE'RE FINISHED!

THE PTHAGUREANS ARE A STUBBORN AND CRUEL RACE, WITHOUT MERCY. IF THEY HAVE DECIDED TO ELIMINATE US, THEY WILL NOT REST UNTIL THEY HAVE DONE SO. THE ONLY REMAINING SOLUTION IS TO FLEE, HIDE IN ANOTHER GALAXY AT THE EDGE OF THE UNIVERSE, AND TRY TO SETTLE DOWN THERE...

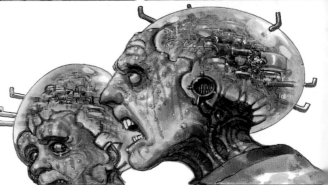

93

STOP! SHOOTING THAT OLD MAN WOULD BE AN INJUSTICE! THERE DOES EXIST A WARRIOR WHO CAN DEFEAT THE METABARON!

TWO PATHETIC LOW-GRADE TECHNO-TECHNO AMBASSADORS WOULD KNOW MORE ABOUT THAT THAN THE EMPIRE'S BEST-INFORMED MENTREKS!

SHOW US YOUR IDENTITY BADGES IMMEDIATELY!

AND IF YOU'RE BLUFFING, I'LL DISINTEGRATE YOUR LYING TONGUE MYSELF, EVEN IF YOU ARE A TECHNO-TECHNO!

I AM BOTH ODA AND HONORATA, OTHON VON SALZA'S WIDOW AND MOTHER OF HIS SON, AGHNAR VON SALZA!

AND WHERE, THEN, DOES YOUR OH-SO-MIGHTY CHAMPION HIDE?

BESIDE ME!

OH, A HOLO-MASK!

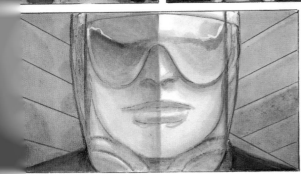

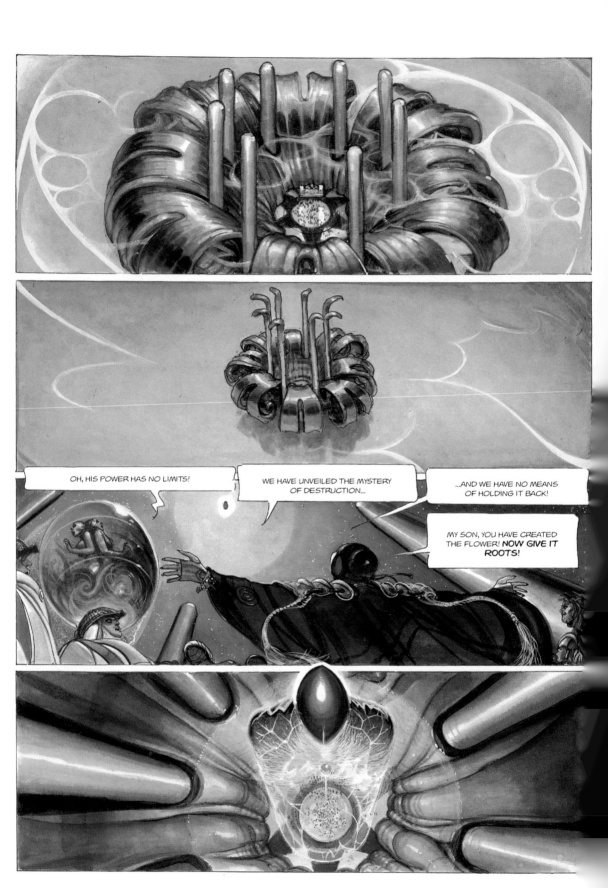

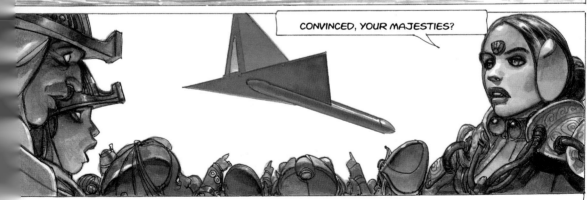

CONVINCED, YOUR MAJESTIES?

AND SO OF COURSE STEELHEAD WAS APPOINTED CHAMPION OF THE HUMAN GALAXY. WITH THE STRONG COMPETITIVE SPIRIT THAT CHARACTERIZED THEIR RACE, THE PTHAGUREANS ROSE TO THE CHALLENGE. THE FOLLOWING DAY, THE DUEL BEGAN...

MILLIONS OF PTHAGUREAN SHIPS AND MILLIONS OF HUMAN SHIPS FORMED AN IMMENSE RING, WITH THE BLACK METACRAFT AND PURPLE METACRAFT IN THE CENTER OF IT, AS FATHER AND SON EMBARKED UPON THE GREATEST BATTLE IN HISTORY.

THAT'S ENOUGH FOR TODAY. WE MUST PRE-PARE DINNER FOR OUR MASTER, WHO COULD BE RETURNING AT ANY MOMENT!

YOU'RE MISTAKEN. IT IS AGHNAR WHO WILL WIN THE BATTLE!

YOU KNOW VERY WELL THAT WE ROBOTS CAN-NOT LIE! I'LL GO ON WITH THE STORY TOMOR-ROW.

JODOROWSKY JIMENEZ ©

OHBOY-OHBOY! WHAT SUSPENSE! I KNOW STEELHEAD IS GOING TO WIN, BECAUSE IF HE DIED, HE COULDN'T HAVE HAD A SON, OUR MASTER'S FATHER!

AGHNAR? IMPOSSIBLE! IF THAT WERE TRUE, OUR GALAXY WOULD NOW BE POPULATED BY PTHAGUREANS AND C MASTER WOULD NOT HAVE BEEN BORN I CAN'T MAKE BIO-HEADS OR BIO-TAILS OUT OF WHAT YOU'RE SAYING!

DAMN! THE SUSPENSE IS CONSTIPATING MY MECA-BOWELS! I NEED SOME TECHNOLAXATIVES NOW!

IN THE COLD LIGHT OF ARTIFICIAL DAWN, THE METABUNKER IS SUSPENDED AS IT HAS BEEN FOR CENTURIES, FORGOTTEN AMID THE RUINS OF THE ONCE FLOURISHING CITY-SHAFT ON TERRA 2014.

I SERVED THE BREAKFAST, IT WENT COLD, I WAITED THE REGULATION TIME, THE METABARON ISN'T EVER COMING BACK!

PLEASE, TONTO, CONTINUE YOUR STORY! YOU BROKE OFF YESTERDAY JUST AS MILLIONS OF PTHAGUREAN AND HUMAN SHIPS WERE AWAITING THE START OF THE DUEL BETWEEN STEELHEAD AND AGHNAR VON SALZA.

TSK! TSK! TSK! SHUT THAT STINKING VALVE YOU CALL YOUR MOUTH, LOTHAR! REGULATION WAITING TIME IS 3:00.00, BUT YOU ONLY WAITED 2:59.991. HYPOCRITICAL RUSTBUCKET!

IN THE TIME TAKEN UP BY YOUR LECTURE, THE REMAINING .009 HAVE PASSED. NOW I CAN DECLARE THAT THE MASTER HAS NOT ARRIVED, AND PUT HIS BREAKFAST INTO THE DISINTEGRATOR! WHY ARE YOU SO CRUEL TO ME, TONTO? COME ON, TELL ME THE STORY...

HUFF! PUFF! SLOW DOWN, THERE'S NO POINT IN CHECKING! ONE ARTIFICIAL NIGHT COULDN'T HAVE DONE IT ANY DAMAGE!

FIRST, WE HAVE TO CHECK THAT THE BIO-ELECTROGRAM IS WORKING.

YOU STUBBORN BIO-TURD! IF YOU DON'T OBEY ME IMMEDIATELY, I'LL DIRECT THE CENTRAL BRAIN TO WIPE OUT YOUR ENTIRE MEMORY-MASS! WE'RE CHECKING!

GULP!

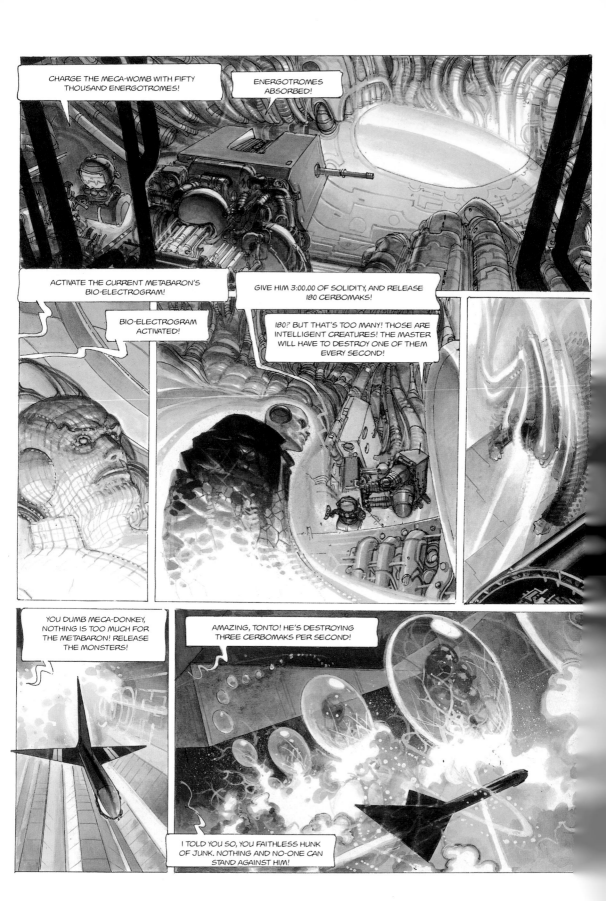

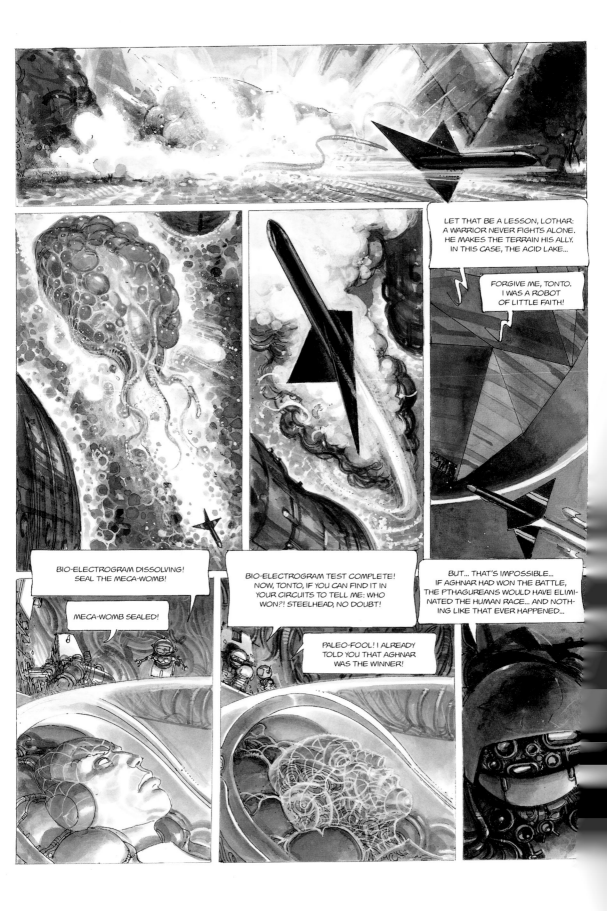

YOUR MULTI-LOGIC IS ONLY APPLICABLE TO YOUR RIGID ROBOTIC SYSTEM. IT MAKES YOU INCAPABLE OF COMPREHENDING THE CHAOS OF A HUMAN PSYCHE. SOMETIMES, ONE WINS BY LOSING! OUT OF PURE PITY, I'LL EXPLAIN HOW...

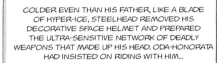

HIS BLOOD RUNNING ICIER THAN THAT OF A VENUSIAN SALMON, ENVELOPED WITHIN HIS INTERIOR SILENCE, AGHNAR, LIKE HIS FATHER BEFORE HIM, CONNECTED THE CONTROL STICK TO HIS GROIN.

COLDER EVEN THAN HIS FATHER, LIKE A BLADE OF HYPER-ICE, STEELHEAD REMOVED HIS DECORATIVE SPACE HELMET AND PREPARED THE ULTRA-SENSITIVE NETWORK OF DEADLY WEAPONS THAT MADE UP HIS HEAD. ODA-HONORATA HAD INSISTED ON RIDING WITH HIM...

"I WANT TO BE BESIDE YOU AT THE MOMENT OF YOUR SUBLIME VICTORY, MY SON. IN KILLING YOUR FATHER, YOU WILL FULFILL THE LEGENDARY TRADITION OF THE METABARONS. A CASTAKA IS NOT A CASTAKA UNTIL HE HAS PROVED HIMSELF MIGHTIER THAN HIS FATHER," SHE TOLD HIM.

THE TWO METACRAFT TOOK THEIR POSITIONS...

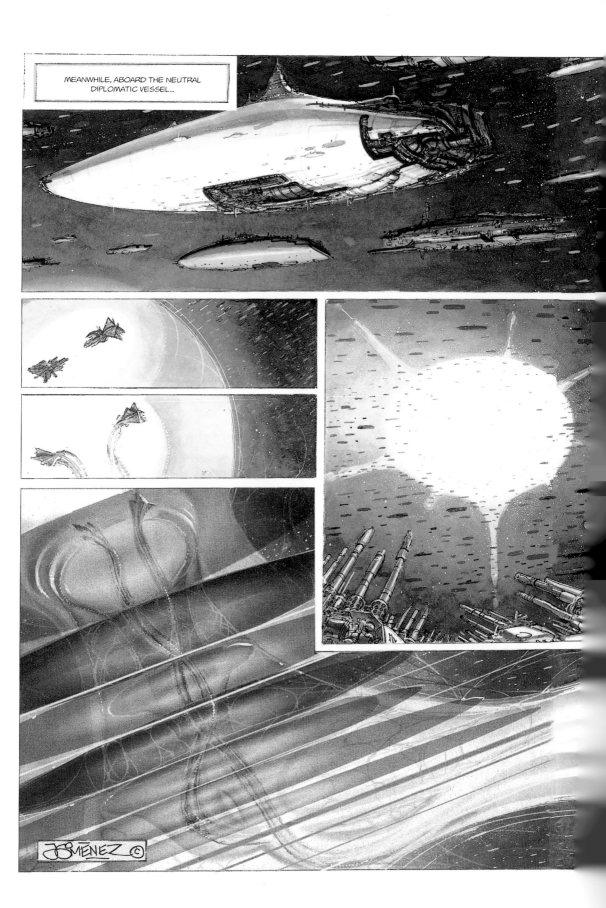

MEANWHILE, ABOARD THE NEUTRAL DIPLOMATIC VESSEL...

THE SUPREME PTHAGUREAN TRIUMVIRATE AND THE IMPERIAL COUPLE JOINTLY GAVE THE SIGNAL TO BEGIN THE MATCH:...

...A FIREWORKS DISPLAY, WHICH NEITHER OF THE WARRIORS, TENSE AS THEY WERE, COULD APPRECIATE...

AS IF ACTING UPON UNSPOKEN ACCORD, THE TWO ADVERSARIES CREATED A BLACK HOLE, WHICH IMMEDIATELY ABSORBED THEM...

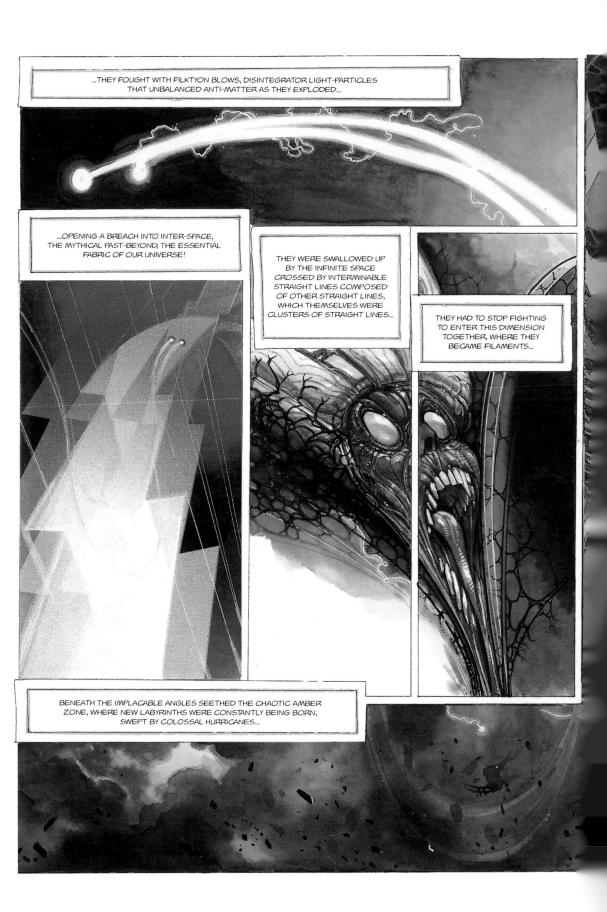

...THEY FOUGHT WITH FILKTYON BLOWS, DISINTEGRATOR LIGHT-PARTICLES THAT UNBALANCED ANTI-MATTER AS THEY EXPLODED...

...OPENING A BREACH INTO INTER-SPACE, THE MYTHICAL PAST-BEYOND, THE ESSENTIAL FABRIC OF OUR UNIVERSE!

THEY WERE SWALLOWED UP BY THE INFINITE SPACE CROSSED BY INTERMINABLE STRAIGHT LINES COMPOSED OF OTHER STRAIGHT LINES, WHICH THEMSELVES WERE CLUSTERS OF STRAIGHT LINES...

THEY HAD TO STOP FIGHTING TO ENTER THIS DIMENSION TOGETHER, WHERE THEY BECAME FILAMENTS...

BENEATH THE IMPLACABLE ANGLES SEETHED THE CHAOTIC AMBER ZONE, WHERE NEW LABYRINTHS WERE CONSTANTLY BEING BORN, SWEPT BY COLOSSAL HURRICANES...

ACCELERATING RECKLESSLY, THEY ONCE AGAIN PENETRATED INTER-SPACE, SPILLING OVER INTO THE DIMENSION OF ORIGINS...

...WHERE ONLY LIVING LIGHTS EXIST, RIPPLING, QUIVERING, RADIATING, GLIMMERING, GLOWING, TWINKLING, AND SPARKLING, LIKE GEMS AS LARGE AS GALAXIES.

A DIMENSION OF PURE BEAUTY AND ETERNAL CALM, WHICH THEY POLLUTED WITH THEIR FEROCIOUS BEAMS!

ON THE BRINK OF MADNESS, TAKING CRAZY RISKS IN THEIR DETERMINATION TO WIN, THEY LET THEIR METACRAFT DEVIATE TOWARDS THE 'OMPHAL', THE MYSTICAL CENTER OF THE BEGINNING AND THE END, WHERE ALL IS CREATED, AND ALL IS CONSUMED...

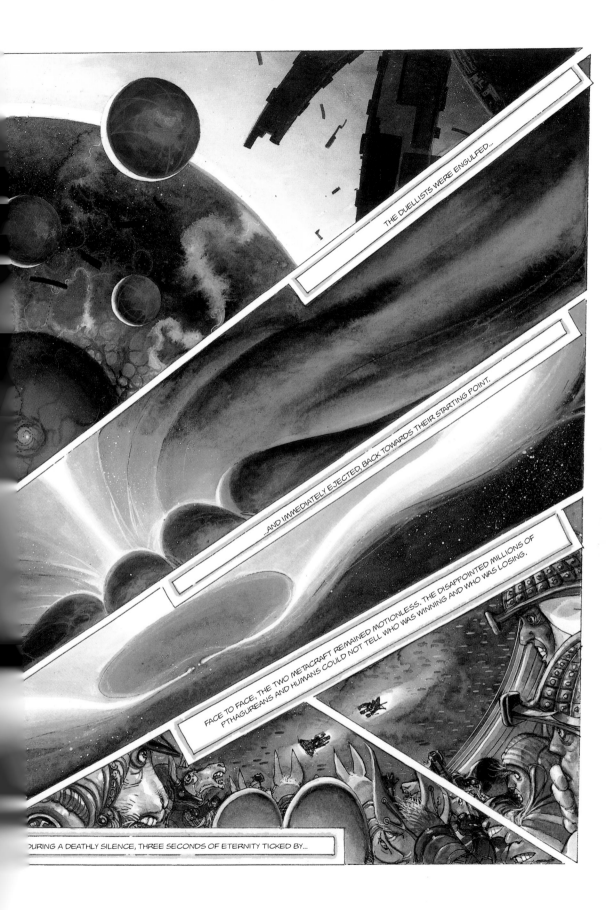

THE DUELLISTS WERE ENGULFED...

...AND IMMEDIATELY EJECTED, BACK TOWARDS THEIR STARTING POINT.

FACE TO FACE, THE TWO METACRAFT REMAINED MOTIONLESS. THE DISAPPOINTED MILLIONS OF PTHAGUREANS AND HUMANS COULD NOT TELL WHO WAS WINNING AND WHO WAS LOSING.

DURING A DEATHLY SILENCE, THREE SECONDS OF ETERNITY TICKED BY...

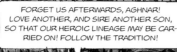

I AM SORRY! I MUST FULFILL MY DUTIES! THE BATTLE WAS AN HONORABLE ONE! YOU WILL DIE PAINLESSLY!

FORGET US AFTERWARDS, AGHNAR! LOVE ANOTHER, AND SIRE ANOTHER SON, SO THAT OUR HEROIC LINEAGE MAY BE CARRIED ON! FOLLOW THE TRADITION!

WHAT...?

MMMMH!

YOU RIDICULOUS GREAT WARRIOR: YOU STILL HAVE FEELINGS! THIS IS THE BODY OF THE WOMAN THAT YOU LOVE AND DESIRE! AND WITHIN IT LIVES YOUR MOTHER'S SPIRIT, WHOM YOU CANNOT HELP LOVING JUST AS MUCH, DESPITE YOUR HATE! I'M GOING TO CARVE HER UP, BIT BY BIT!

YOU SHAME ME, PATHETIC TRAITOR! YOU'RE JUST A BIO-RAT, NOT A WARRIOR! YOU DISGRACE OUR CODE OF HONOR!

PALEO-FANTASIES! ALL THAT MATTERS IS WINNING, AND ANY WEAPON MAY BE USED TO THAT END! AT THIS MOMENT MY WEAPON IS YOUR MOTHER HONORATA, CONTAINED IN THE BODY OF YOUR WIFE ODA!

WHO IS ALSO YOUR MOTHER!

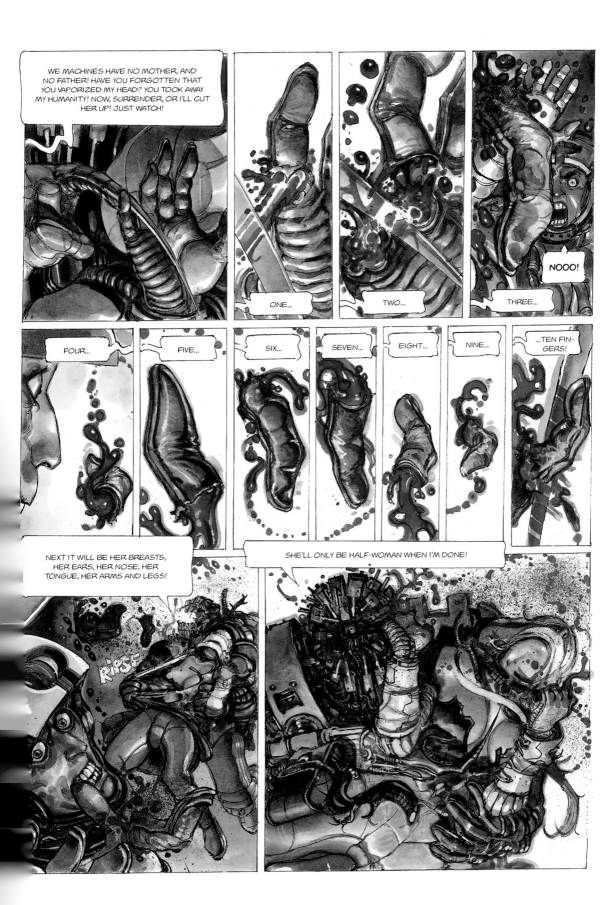

I FORGIVE YOU, HONORATA! ONLY YOUR LOVE FOR MY FATHER MADE YOU ACT THE WAY YOU DID!

AND THE TWO OF THEM, IN UNISON, SET OFF THE MINI-BOMBS INSIDE THEIR BODIES. THE GALAXY NEVER WITNESSED A MORE BEAUTIFUL EXPLOSION!

OOO! OOO! OOO! WHAT A GRAND FINALE! TWO TITANS, SHARING A DEATH FOR SACRED HEROES. BUT... I DON'T UNDERSTAND... IT COULDN'T HAVE BEEN POSSIBLE FOR THE CONTEMPTIBLE STEELHEAD, SHAMED BEFORE ALL HUMANITY, TO CARRY ON THE GLORIOUS CLAN OF THE METABARONS! SO? HOW WAS OUR MASTER BORN?

YOU LACK BOTH PATIENCE AND IMAGINATION! THAT FIEND WAS OF COURSE UNANIMOUSLY DESPISED, BUT... HIS STORY DOES NOT END THERE. IN FACT IT'S ONLY THE BEGINNING... SHUT YOUR REPULSIVE ORAL GRATE AND LISTEN:...

HUMANITY WAS SAVED. BUT IT WAS ALSO
THE END OF THE PTHAGUREAN RACE.

YOUR MAJESTIES, THE ALIEN SAID:
"TO ALL PTHAGUREAN SHIPS: IMMEDIATE
COLLECTIVE SUICIDE! ENACT!"

VII KUMS PTHAGUROS:
SUIIRFIIN TOUNGS FANAK! UNG!

TRUE TO THEIR WORD, THE INVADERS COMMITTED SUICIDE, OUTLINING A RING OF FIRE ACROSS
THE INFINITE COSMOS.

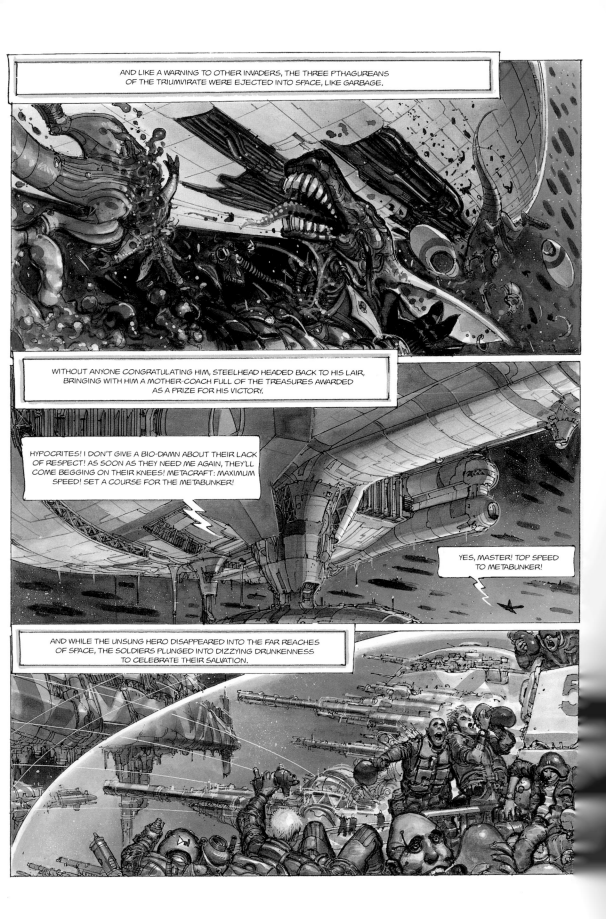

AND LIKE A WARNING TO OTHER INVADERS, THE THREE PTHAGUREANS OF THE TRIUMVIRATE WERE EJECTED INTO SPACE, LIKE GARBAGE.

WITHOUT ANYONE CONGRATULATING HIM, STEELHEAD HEADED BACK TO HIS LAIR, BRINGING WITH HIM A MOTHER-COACH FULL OF THE TREASURES AWARDED AS A PRIZE FOR HIS VICTORY.

HYPOCRITES! I DON'T GIVE A BIO-DAMN ABOUT THEIR LACK OF RESPECT! AS SOON AS THEY NEED ME AGAIN, THEY'LL COME BEGGING ON THEIR KNEES! METACRAFT: MAXIMUM SPEED! SET A COURSE FOR THE METABUNKER!

YES, MASTER! TOP SPEED TO METABUNKER!

AND WHILE THE UNSUNG HERO DISAPPEARED INTO THE FAR REACHES OF SPACE, THE SOLDIERS PLUNGED INTO DIZZYING DRUNKENNESS TO CELEBRATE THEIR SALVATION.

...INCLUDING THE IMPERIAL COUPLE'S!

MEANWHILE, DRIFTING ACROSS THE DESERTS OF SIRTHA, WITHIN THE SOLITUDE OF THE METABUNKER...

...STEELHEAD WAS TRYING ON COSTUME HELMETS TO MASK THE NETWORK OF DEADLY WEAPONS THAT MADE UP HIS HEAD!

WHAT DO YOU THINK OF THIS ONE, TONTO?

I'M RECEIVING A SPECIAL GALACTIC TRANSMISSION FROM THE NEW GOLDEN PALACE! THEY URGENTLY REQUEST AN AUDIENCE!

I KNEW IT! THEY NEED ME! MY TIME HAS COME! I WANT THEM ON THEIR KNEES! TONTO, ACTIVATE THE HOLO-DISPLAY!

TOO POETIC FOR A WARRIOR, MASTER! IT WOULD BE BETTER SUITED TO THE ROMANTIC OCTOPUS OF THE HYPERTUBE!"

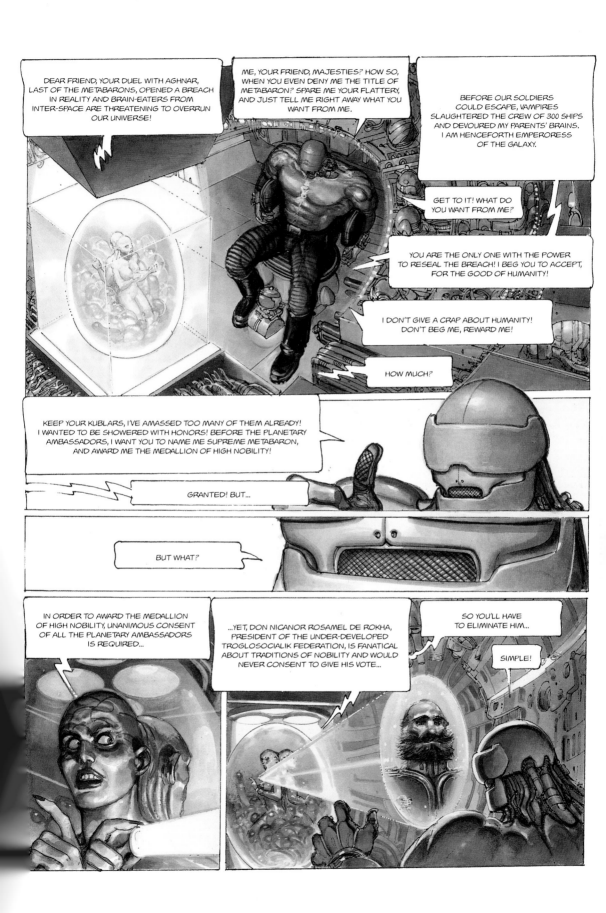

DEAR FRIEND, YOUR DUEL WITH AGHNAR, LAST OF THE METABARONS, OPENED A BREACH IN REALITY AND BRAIN-EATERS FROM INTER-SPACE ARE THREATENING TO OVERRUN OUR UNIVERSE!

ME, YOUR FRIEND, MAJESTIES? HOW SO, WHEN YOU EVEN DENY ME THE TITLE OF METABARON? SPARE ME YOUR FLATTERY, AND JUST TELL ME RIGHT AWAY WHAT YOU WANT FROM ME.

BEFORE OUR SOLDIERS COULD ESCAPE, VAMPIRES SLAUGHTERED THE CREW OF 300 SHIPS AND DEVOURED MY PARENTS' BRAINS. I AM HENCEFORTH EMPERORESS OF THE GALAXY.

GET TO IT! WHAT DO YOU WANT FROM ME?

YOU ARE THE ONLY ONE WITH THE POWER TO RESEAL THE BREACH! I BEG YOU TO ACCEPT, FOR THE GOOD OF HUMANITY!

I DON'T GIVE A CRAP ABOUT HUMANITY! DON'T BEG ME, REWARD ME!

HOW MUCH?

KEEP YOUR KUBLARS, I'VE AMASSED TOO MANY OF THEM ALREADY! I WANTED TO BE SHOWERED WITH HONORS! BEFORE THE PLANETARY AMBASSADORS, I WANT YOU TO NAME ME SUPREME METABARON, AND AWARD ME THE MEDALLION OF HIGH NOBILITY!

GRANTED! BUT...

BUT WHAT?

IN ORDER TO AWARD THE MEDALLION OF HIGH NOBILITY, UNANIMOUS CONSENT OF ALL THE PLANETARY AMBASSADORS IS REQUIRED...

...YET, DON NICANOR ROSAMEL DE ROKHA, PRESIDENT OF THE UNDER-DEVELOPED TROGLOSOCIALIK FEDERATION, IS FANATICAL ABOUT TRADITIONS OF NOBILITY AND WOULD NEVER CONSENT TO GIVE HIS VOTE...

SO YOU'LL HAVE TO ELIMINATE HIM...

SIMPLE!

123

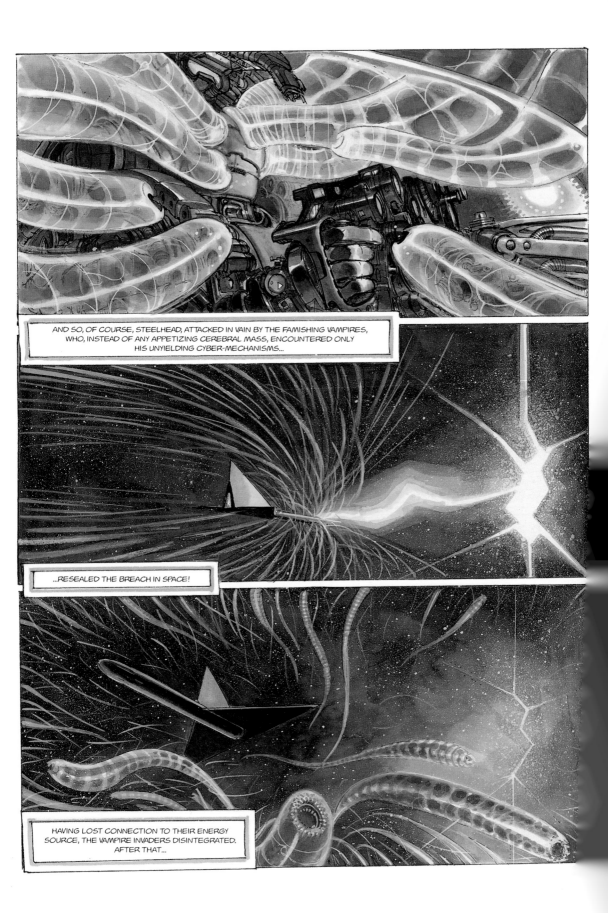

AND SO, OF COURSE, STEELHEAD, ATTACKED IN VAIN BY THE FAMISHING VAMPIRES, WHO, INSTEAD OF ANY APPETIZING CEREBRAL MASS, ENCOUNTERED ONLY HIS UNYIELDING CYBER-MECHANISMS...

...RESEALED THE BREACH IN SPACE!

HAVING LOST CONNECTION TO THEIR ENERGY SOURCE, THE VAMPIRE INVADERS DISINTEGRATED. AFTER THAT...

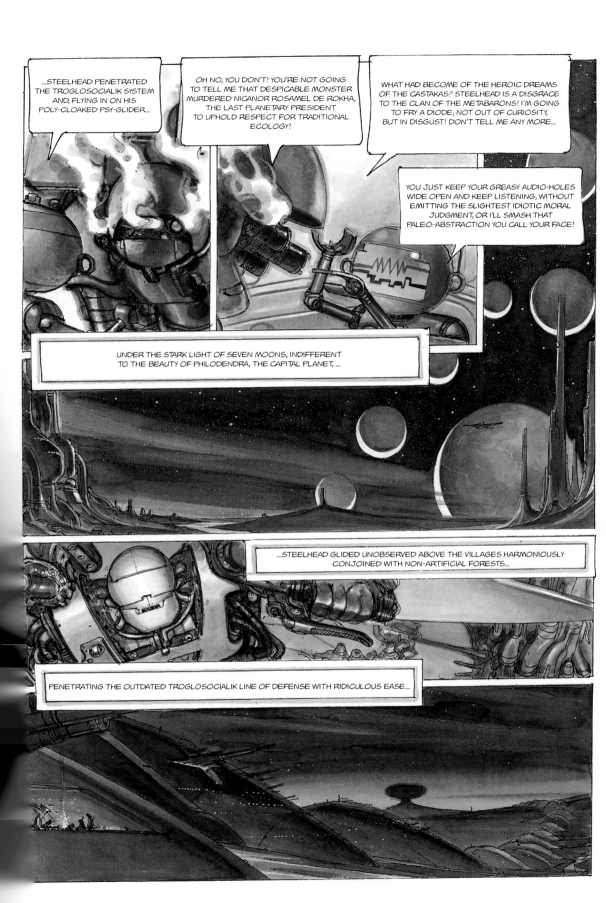

...STEELHEAD PENETRATED THE TROGLOSOCIALIK SYSTEM AND, FLYING IN ON HIS POLY-CLOAKED PSY-GLIDER...

OH NO, YOU DON'T! YOU'RE NOT GOING TO TELL ME THAT DESPICABLE MONSTER MURDERED NICANOR ROSAMEL DE ROKHA, THE LAST PLANETARY PRESIDENT TO UPHOLD RESPECT FOR TRADITIONAL ECOLOGY!

WHAT HAD BECOME OF THE HEROIC DREAMS OF THE CASTAKAS? STEELHEAD IS A DISGRACE TO THE CLAN OF THE METABARONS! I'M GOING TO FRY A DIODE, NOT OUT OF CURIOSITY, BUT IN DISGUST! DON'T TELL ME ANY MORE...

YOU JUST KEEP YOUR GREASY AUDIO-HOLES WIDE OPEN AND KEEP LISTENING, WITHOUT EMITTING THE SLIGHTEST IDIOTIC MORAL JUDGMENT, OR I'LL SMASH THAT PALEO-ABSTRACTION YOU CALL YOUR FACE!

UNDER THE STARK LIGHT OF SEVEN MOONS, INDIFFERENT TO THE BEAUTY OF PHILODENDRA, THE CAPITAL PLANET, ...

...STEELHEAD GLIDED UNOBSERVED ABOVE THE VILLAGES HARMONIOUSLY CONJOINED WITH NON-ARTIFICIAL FORESTS...

PENETRATING THE OUTDATED TROGLOSOCIALIK LINE OF DEFENSE WITH RIDICULOUS EASE...

125

...HE ARRIVED AT THE HALERCE TREE, FAMOUS FOR BEING THE OLDEST TREE IN THE GALAXY...
A VENERABLE GIANT OF GOLDEN SINGING LEAVES, WHICH STRUCK UP A RESONANT HYMN FOR THE THREE RISING SUNS!

BUT AS HE APPROACHED, HE SAW THAT THE GOLDEN LEAVES WERE REALLY MILLIONS OF DYUKKA-BIRDS,
TINY LEGENDARY BIRDS THAT SANG WITH VOICES AS PURE AS CASTRATAS'.

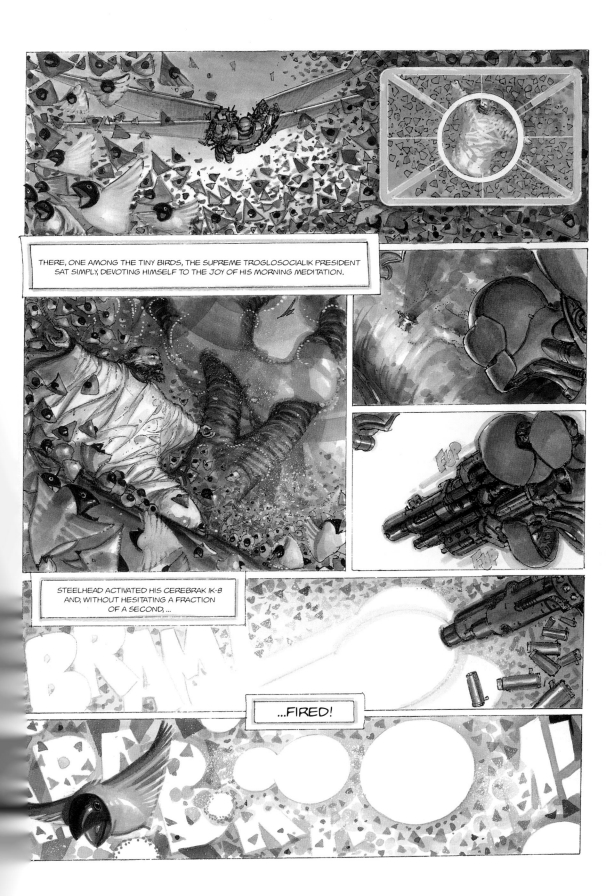

THERE, ONE AMONG THE TINY BIRDS, THE SUPREME TROGLOSOCIALIK PRESIDENT SAT SIMPLY, DEVOTING HIMSELF TO THE JOY OF HIS MORNING MEDITATION.

STEELHEAD ACTIVATED HIS CEREBRAK IK-8 AND, WITHOUT HESITATING A FRACTION OF A SECOND, ...

...FIRED!

127

BY UNANIMOUS AGREEMENT OF ALL
THE PLANETARY AMBASSADORS, WE AWARD
THIS MEDALLION OF HIGH NOBILITY...

...TO THE DISTINGUISHED SUPREME METABARON,
FOR HAVING TWICE SAVED HUMANITY
FROM COMPLETE ANNIHILATION!

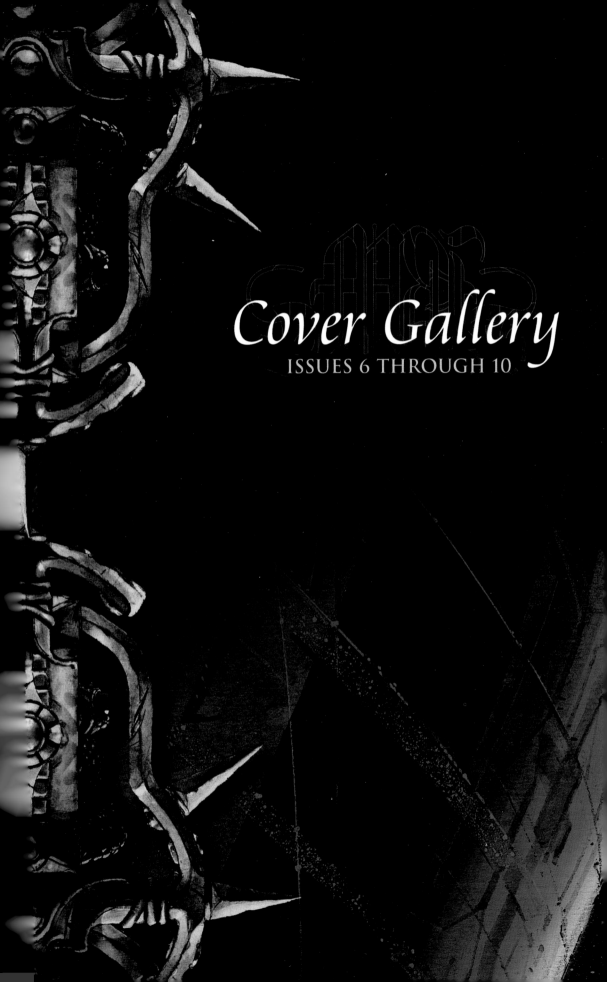

Cover Gallery

ISSUES 6 THROUGH 10

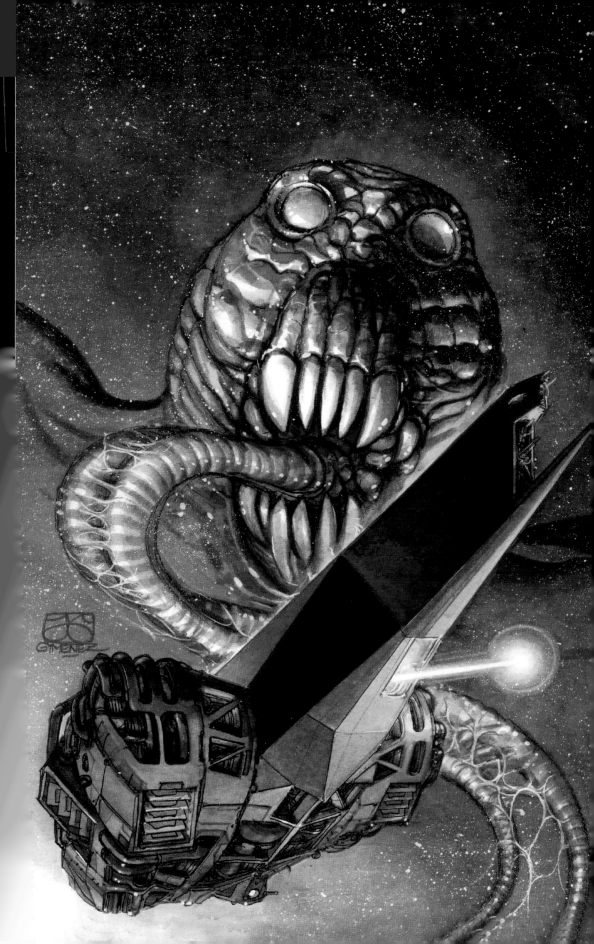

Other Great Books from Humanoids Publishing™

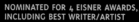

SON OF THE GUN: BORN IN THE TRASH
By Jodorowsky and Bess

In the South American city of Huatuclo, a baby is born with a tail. Survival is almost impossible in this city of the dammed, but for someone with a deformity like Juan's, chances are almost zero. Almost. Juan's ascension from the slums will cost him his soul, and finding redemption may cost him his life.

Hardcover album, Full Color, 56 pages, $14.95

FROM CLOUD 99 MEMORIES PART I & II
by Yslaire

With story, art, and cover by Yslaire (who was nominated for FOUR 2000 Eisner Awards for Memories Part I). The first volume of this three-part series tells the story of Eva Stern, a 98-year-old psychoanalyst, who receives strange anonymous e-mail. It features a series of altered photographs that seem to have no apparent link except for the fact that they depict tragic events of the 20th Century and the almost obsessive representation of flying beings. In From Cloud 99 Memories Part II , we learn more about the flying beings that are linked to the e-mails a now ailing Eva Stern has been receiving. The situation grows more complex as one mysterious being in particular is found in more historical pictures than just the ones in the e-mails. Contains Nudity. Not For Children.

Hardcover album, Full Color, 64 pages, $14.95

THE TECHNOPRIESTS #3:
PLANETA GAMES
Art and covers by Janjetov and BeltranStory
by Jodorowsky

Albino must undergo many trials before becoming the Supreme TechnoPriest, master of games and virtual reality. From his birth on the Sacred Asteroid, to his violation of the highest cybernetic access levels, he recounts his rise to glory amid the din and clamor of a cosmic struggle. A tale of the power of dreams.

Hardcover album, Full Color, 56 pages, $14.95

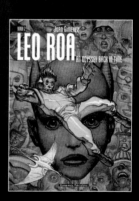

LEO ROA, BOOK 2:
AN ODYSSEY BACK IN TIME
By Juan Gimenez

An outstanding adventure, filled with action and intrigue, written and illustrated by Metabarons artist, Juan Gimenez. Leo Roa is accidentally sent hurtling through the ages when an attempt to capture a group of terrorists collides with a time travel experiment. World War II fighter planes and dinosaurs play a part in this stand-alone story.

Hardcover album, Full Color, 60 pages, $14.95

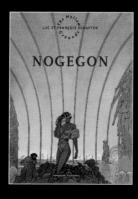

NOGEGON
By Luc & Francois Schuiten

The logic behind the world of the hollow grounds seems familiar to us, but is in fact a vertiginous trap. It becomes a real treat for the attentive reader to let himself slide into these chasms where elegance is just a discreet mask concealing the most terrible of weapons: intelligence.

Hardcover album, Full Color, 72 pages, $14.95

Other Great Comics